EEK
&ACK

EEK DISCOVERS EARTH

written by
BLAKE A. HOENA

illustrations by
STEVE HARPSTER

Raintree

Raintree is an imprint of Capstone Global Library Limited, a company incorporated in England and Wales having its registered office at 7 Pilgrim Street, London, EC4V 6LB – Registered company number: 6695582

www.raintreepublishers.co.uk
myorders@raintreepublishers.co.uk

ISBN 978 1 406 27565 0
17 16 15 14 13
10 9 8 7 6 5 4 3 2 1

British Library Cataloguing in Publication Data
A full catalogue record for this book is available from the British Library.

Printed in China by Nordica.
1013/CA21301916

TABLE OF CONTENTS

Chapter 1

EEK FINDS A PLANET

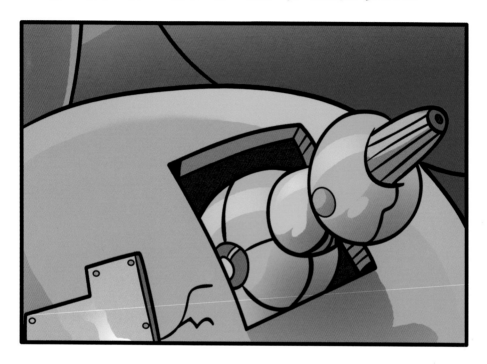

"Eek, what are you doing with Dad's laser?" Ack asked.

"Shhh," Eek hushed his little brother. "Don't say anything."

"But he doesn't like it when you zap things," Ack said.

"I know. I know," Eek whispered. "But I found this strange green and blue planet. Look!"

"Wow!" Ack exclaimed. "What's it called?"

"Earth," Eek replied. "Silly, huh?"

"Yeah," Ack laughed. "Why don't we call it Dirt?"

"Or Ground," Eek added with a chuckle.

"Or Mud," Ack said with a snort. "Gloop is a much better name for a planet."

Eek and Ack studied Earth a bit more closely.

"Look at the goofy things earthlings do," Ack said.

"Yeah, they talk to these little square robots all day," Eek said.

"And they wash their underwear in spaceships," Ack added.

"Earthlings should be vaporized," Eek growled.

"Can I do it?" Ack asked. "Please?"

"No! I found Earth!" Eek shouted. "Go find your own planet to zap."

Chapter 2

EEK AND ACK GET CAUGHT

Eek and Ack's dad was in the kitchen eating a slimewich and drinking Solar Cola. He heard his sons arguing.

"Eek! Ack!" he yelled. "What are you doing in my laser room?"

Eek and Ack panicked. They didn't want to get in trouble.

"We're not vaporizing anything," Ack replied.

"Shhh," Eek growled at his brother.

"Boys, you shouldn't zap every planet you find," Dad said. "There won't be any left for other space aliens to conquer."

"Awww," Eek whined.

"You two destroy everything. I want you to try making something for a change," Dad said.

"Okay, Dad," said Ack, nodding.

Eek said nothing.

Eek and Ack walked outside. Eek
looked deep in thought.

"What are we going to build?" Ack
asked.

"A spaceship," Eek said.

"A spaceship? Why?" Ack asked.

"Then we can go conquer Earth!" Eek exclaimed.

"But Dad said–" Ack began.

"He said to make something," Eek growled. "So that's what we are doing."

Ack gulped nervously.

Chapter 3

EEK'S SPACESHIP

"Hand me that tool," Eek said.

Ack watched as Eek twisted wires and tightened bolts.

"Is the ship ready yet?" Ack asked.

"No, no. I need to put in the whizzler drive," Eek explained. "Now hand me that blue tool there."

Ack watched as Eek turned screws and hammered nails. It was boring, but Ack tried to be patient.

"Now is it ready?" Ack asked.

Eek leaped into the spaceship.

"It is," Eek said. "And it's time to conquer Earth!"

Ack gulped nervously.

"Ack, begin the countdown," Eek said.

"Okay, ten, nine, eight . . . um . . ." Ack paused. "What comes after eight? I always forget."

"Grrr," Eek growled. "Just blast off!"

Rumble, rumble!

Eek's spaceship shot into space.
Eek and Ack zipped across the
universe. Soon, they saw the
planet Earth.

Ack landed the spaceship inside the Sudsy Duck Laundrette.

"Look at those silly earthlings," Eek said.

"Yeah, who folds their underwear?" Ack said.

Meanwhile, a little girl spotted Eek and Ack's spaceship.

"Daddy, no one's using that washing machine," she said.

"Go put our last load in it," her dad said.

The little girl picked up a basket full of dirty, smelly clothes. She dumped it into Eek and Ack's spaceship.

"Ew, gross!" they shouted together.

"Earthlings are attacking us with stinky socks and underwear!" Ack screamed.

"They are more evil than I thought," Eek growled. "Hit the emergency blast-off button!"

Rumble, rumble!

"I think Dad's going to be mad," Ack said as they flew off.

"Why? We didn't destroy much," Eek replied.

"But we're bringing home all this dirty laundry for him to wash," Ack said.

"Grr," Eek growled.

ABOUT THE AUTHOR

Blake Hoena has written more than 20 books
for children. He once spent a whole weekend
just watching his favourite science-fiction films.
Those films made him wonder if he could invent
some aliens who had death rays, hyperdrives, and
clever equipment, but still couldn't conquer Earth.
That's when he created the two young aliens Eek
and Ack, who play at conquering Earth just like
earthling children play at beating villains.

ABOUT THE ARTIST

Steve Harpster has loved to draw funny cartoons,
mean monsters, and goofy gadgets ever since he
first starting using a pencil. At school, he preferred
drawing pictures for stories rather than writing them.
Steve now draws funny pictures for books as his job,
and that's really what he's best at. Steve lives in Ohio
in America and has a sheepdog called Doodle.

GLOSSARY

conquer to defeat and take control of an enemy; Eek always wants to conquer planet Earth.

earthling a creature from the planet Earth

growled made a low deep noise

laser a device that makes a very narrow, powerful beam of light

panicked filled with fear or worry

vaporized turned something into very small particles. Space aliens vaporize things with lasers.

whined complained or made drawn-out sounds that are sad or unpleasant

whizzler drive a machine on planet Gloop that makes alien spaceships go very fast

TALK ABOUT THE STORY

1. Eek and Ack thought the earthlings acted strangely. Can you think of other things that earthlings do that might seem weird to the aliens?

2. Do you think that Eek and Ack did what their dad wanted them to do? Explain your answer.

3. Eek and Ack built a spaceship. Have you ever built anything?

WRITING TIME

1. The author of this book sometimes creates items that are unique to the planet Gloop. Create your own item that is only found on planet Gloop. What is its name and what does it do?

2. Imagine that the little girl at the laundrette had seen Eek and Ack. What would she have done? Write about it.

3. Write one more chapter to go at the end of this book. Write about what Eek and Ack's dad says when he sees all the dirty clothes they have brought back home.

EXPLORING THE UNIVERSE

with Eek & Ack

Eek and Ack love spending time in their dad's laser room. A laser is a device that makes a very narrow, but powerful, beam of light. Lasers are used in many machines familiar to humans. Here are a few:

• CD and DVD players use lasers to read the data that is stored on the discs.

- When you're shopping, the sales assistant may pass the things you buy over a special light. This is a laser that reads the barcodes that are found on price tags or the products themselves. Barcodes tell the till how much something costs.

- Doctors sometimes use lasers to do surgery. Laser surgery is common on eyes, for example.

- Lasers are used in clothing factories to cut through hundreds of layers of fabric at once.

THE FUN DOESN'T STOP HERE!

DISCOVER MORE AT...
WWW.RAINTREEPUBLISHERS.CO.UK